Traces

Paula Fox

ILLUSTRATED BY
Karla Kuskin

FRONT STREET
Asheville, North Carolina

LIBRARY OF CONGRESS CATALOGING-IN-PUBLICATION DATA
Fox, Paula.
Traces / Paula Fox ; illustrated by Karla Kuskin.
p. cm.
Summary: Looks at the traces left behind by a turtle on the sand,
a jet in the sky, and even a long-gone dinosaur in loose soil.
ISBN-13: 978-1-932425-43-7 (hardcover : alk. paper)
[1. Nature—Fiction.] I. Kuskin, Karla, ill. II. Title.
PZ7.F838Tra 2008
[E]—dc22   2006011739

FRONT STREET
An Imprint of Boyds Mills Press, Inc.
815 Church Street
Honesdale, Pennsylvania 18431

For Katie and Alexander King, Jacob and Gabriel Senn, and Maria Fox Menely

P.F.

To Paula and Martin with love, and to Nick Kuskin, who stepped in
as art director and took over when it was most helpful to do so.
And also to Jannet Lynch, who worked hard and long on these pages
that needed smart, fresh hands, with thanks and more love

K.K.

Something, someone was just here.

Now there's barely a trace of it in the lily pond,

only bubbles of water and air.

Plump, wattled, warty, croaking

is the bullfrog that left its traces in the lily pond.

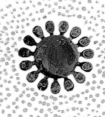

Something, someone was just here.

Now there's barely a trace of it ...

except for a flash of its brush.

Sleek, quick, furry, sharp-nosed

is the fox that left its trace

in a glade in the woods.

Something, someone was just here.

Now there's barely a trace of it,

except for the path it made . . .

across the sand to the sea.

A little turtle
leaves its trace
on the sand
as it drags its way
to the sea.

Four little legs,
one darting head,
shelled and plodding
itself in its own house.

Something, someone was just here.

Now there's barely a trace of it …

in the tall wild grass.

Slithering, quivering, curling, straightening,

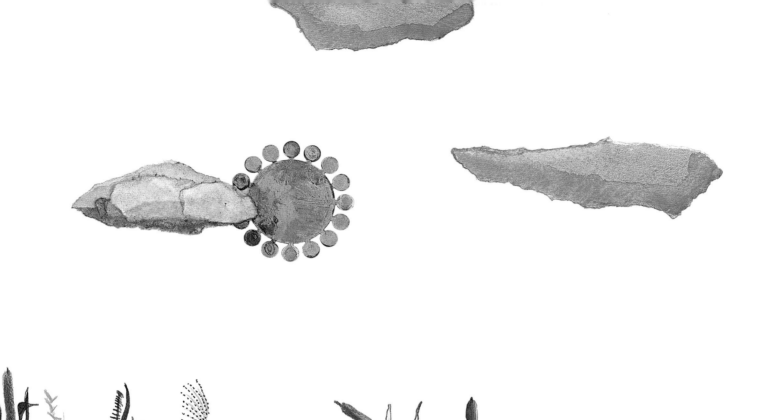

a snake has left a trace in the tall wild grass.

Something, someone was just here.

Now there's barely a trace of it across the sky.

Straight as two arrows, already dissolving,

a jet plane has left its traces across the sky.

Something, someone was just here.
Now there's barely a trace of it
under the window to the garden.

Wriggly, squirming, slimy, slippery . . .

a snail has left its trace beneath the garden window.

Something, someone was once here.

Now there's barely a trace of it

in a cliff of rock and loose soil.

Massive, three-toed, ancient,
a dinosaur has left its traces
in a cliff of rock and loose soil.

They were just here.

Now there are still shadows on the ground.

Following the leader,

the children formed a line along the low stone wall.

It's late in the day. Soon they'll be called to their suppers.

Someone, something was just here.

It has left its traces in leaves flying,

tree branches bending, scraps of paper waving.

The wind!

The invisible wind

that

can only be seen

in

its

traces.